The Scalp Hunter, and War on Bear Creek

Robert E. Howard

The Scalp Hunter

The reason I am giving the full facts of this here affair is to refute a lot of rumors which is circulating about me. I am sick and tired of these lies about me terrorizing the town of Grizzly Claw and ruining their wagon-yard just for spite and trying to murder all their leading citizens. They is more'n one side to anything. These folks which is going around telling about me knocking the mayor of Grizzly Claw down a flight of steps with a kitchen stove ain't yet added that the mayor was trying to blast me with a sawed-off shotgun. As for saying that all I done was with malice afore-thought–if I was a hot-headed man like some I know, I could easy lose my temper over this here slander, but being shy and retiring by nature, I keeps my dignity and merely remarks that these gossipers is blamed liars, and I will kick the ears off of them if I catch them.

I warn't even going to Grizzly Claw in the first place. I'm kind of particular where I go to. I'd been in the settlements along Wild River for several weeks, tending to my own business, and I was headed for Pistol Mountain, when I seen "Tunk" Willoughby setting on a log at the forks where the trail to Grizzly Claw splits off of the Pistol Mountain road. Tunk ain't got no more sense than the law allows anyway, and now he looked plumb discouraged. He had a mangled ear, a couple of black eyes, and a lump on his head so big his hat wouldn't fit. From time to time he spit out a tooth.

I pulled up Cap'n Kidd and said: "What kind of a brawl have you been into?"

"I been to Grizzly Claw," he said, just like that explained it. But I didn't get the drift, because I hadn't never been to Grizzly Claw.

"That's the meanest town in these mountains," he said. "They ain't got no real law there, but they got a feller which claims to be a officer, and if you so much as spit, he says you bust a law and has got to pay a fine. If you puts up a holler, the citizens comes to his assistance. You see what happened to me. I never found out just

1

what law I was supposed to broke," Tunk said, "but it must of been one they was particular fond of. I give 'em a good fight as long as they confined theirselves to rocks and gun butts, but when they interjuiced fence rails and wagon-tongues into the fray, I give up the ghost."

"What you go there for, anyhow?" I demanded.

"Well," he said, mopping off some dried blood, "I was lookin' for you. Three or four days ago I was in the vicinity of Bear Creek, and yore cousin Jack Gordon told me somethin' to tell you."

Him showing no sign of going on, I said: "Well, what was it?"

"I cain't remember," he said. "That lammin' they gimme in Grizzly Claw has plumb addled my brains. Jack told me to tell you to keep a sharp look-out for somebody, but I cain't remember who, or why. But somebody had did somethin' awful to somebody on Bear Creek– seems like it was yore Uncle Jeppard Grimes."

"But why did you go to Grizzly Claw?" I demanded. "I warn't there."

"I dunno," he said. "Seems like the feller which Jack wanted you to get was from Grizzly Claw, or was supposed to go there, or somethin'."

"A great help you be!" I said in disgust. "Here somebody has went and wronged one of my kinfolks, maybe, and you forgets the details. Try to remember the name of the feller, anyway. If I knew who he was, I could lay him out, and then find out what he did later on. Think, can't you?"

"Did you ever have a wagon-tongue busted over yore head?" he said. "I tell you, it's just right recent that I remembered my own name. It was all I could do to rekernize you just now. If you'll come back in a couple of days, maybe by then I'll remember what all Jack told me."

2

I give a snort of disgust and turned off the road and headed up the trail for Grizzly Claw. I thought maybe I could learn something there. If somebody had done dirt to Uncle Jeppard, I wanted to know it. Us Bear Creek folks may fight amongst ourselves, but we stands for no stranger to impose on any one of us. Uncle Jeppard was about as old as the Humbolt Mountains, and he'd fit Indians for a living in his younger days. He was still a tough old knot. Anybody that could do him a wrong and get away with it, sure wasn't no ordinary man, so it wasn't no wonder that word had been sent out for me to get on his trail. And now I hadn't no idea who to look for, or why, just because of Tunk Willoughby's weak skull. I despise these here egg-headed weaklings.

WELL, I ARROVE IN GRIZZLY Claw late in the afternoon and went first to the wagon-yard and seen that Cap'n Kidd was put in a good stall and fed proper, and warned the fellow there to keep away from him if he didn't want his brains kicked out. Cap'n Kidd has a disposition like a shark and he don't like strangers. It warn't much of a wagon-yard, and there was only five other horses there, besides me and Cap'n Kidd–a pinto, bay, and piebald, and a couple of pack-horses.

I then went back into the business part of the village, which was one dusty street with stores and saloons on each side, and I didn't pay much attention to the town, because I was trying to figure out how I could go about trying to find out what I wanted to know, and couldn't think of no questions to ask nobody about nothing.

Well, I was approaching a saloon called the Apache Queen, and was looking at the ground in meditation, when I seen a silver dollar laying in the dust close to a hitching rack. I immediately stooped down and picked it up, not noticing how close it was to the hind laigs of a mean-looking mule. When I stooped over he hauled off and kicked me in the head. Then he let out a awful bray and commenced jumping around holding up his hind hoof, and some men come running out of the saloon, and one of 'em hollered: "He's tryin' to kill my mule! Call the law!"

Quite a crowd gathered and the feller which owned the mule hollered like a catamount. He was a mean-looking cuss with mournful whiskers and a cock-eye. He yelled like somebody was stabbing him, and I couldn't get in a word edge-ways. Then a feller with a long skinny neck and two guns come up and said: "I'm the sheriff, what's goin' on here? Who is this big feller? What's he done?"

The whiskered cuss hollered: "He kicked hisself in the head with my mule and crippled the pore critter for life! I demands my rights! He's got to pay me three hundred and fifty dollars for my mule!"

"Aw," I said, "that mule ain't hurt none; his leg's just kinda numbed. Anyway, I ain't got but five bucks, and whoever gets them will take 'em offa my dead body." I then hitched my six-guns forwards, and the crowd kinda fell away.

"I demands that you 'rest him!" howled Drooping-whiskers. "He tried to 'sassinate my mule!"

"You ain't got no star," I told the feller which said he was the law. "You ain't goin' to arrest me."

"Does you dast resist arrest?" he said, fidgeting with his belt.

"Who said anything about resistin' arrest?" I retorted. "All I aim to do is see how far your neck will stretch before it breaks."

"Don't you dast lay hands on a officer of the law!" he squawked, backing away in a hurry.

I was tired of talking and thirsty, so I merely give a snort and turned away through the crowd towards a saloon pushing 'em right and left out of my way. I saw 'em gang up in the street, talking low and mean, but I give no heed.

They wasn't nobody in the saloon except the barman and a gangling cowpuncher which had draped hisself over the bar. I ordered whiskey and when I had drank a few fingers of the rottenest muck I believe I ever tasted, I give it up in disgust and throwed the dollar on the bar which I had found, and was starting out when the barkeeper hollered:

"Hey!"

I turned around and said courteously: "Don't you yell at me like that, you bat-eared buzzard! What you want?"

"This here dollar ain't no good!" he said, banging it on the bar.

"Well, neither is your whiskey," I snarled, because I was getting mad. "So that makes us even!"

I am a long-suffering man but it looked like everybody in Grizzly Claw was out to gyp the stranger in their midst.

"You can't run no blazer over me!" he hollered. "You gimme a real dollar, or else–"

He ducked down behind the bar and come up with a shotgun so I taken it away from him and bent the barrel double across my knee and throwed it after him as he run out the back door hollering help, murder.

The cowpuncher had picked up the dollar and bit on it, and then he looked at me very sharp, and said: "Where did you get this?"

"I found it, if it's any of your dern business," I snapped, because I was mad. Saying no more I strode out the door, and the minute I hit the street somebody let *bam!* at me from behind a rain-barrel across the street and shot my hat off. So I slammed a bullet back through the barrel and the feller hollered and fell out in the open yelling blue murder. It was the feller which called hisself the sheriff and he was drilled through the hind laig. I noticed a lot of heads sticking up over window sills and around doors, so I roared: "Let that be a warnin' to you Grizzly Claw coyotes! I'm Breckinridge Elkins from Bear Creek up in the Humbolts, and I shoot better in my sleep than most men does wide awake!"

I then lent emphasis to my remarks by punctuating a few signboards and knocking out a few winder panes and everybody hollered and ducked. So I shoved my guns back in their scabbards and went into a restaurant. The citizens come out from their hiding-places and carried off my victim, and he made more noise over a broke laig than I thought was possible for a grown man.

There was some folks in the restaurant but they stampeded out the back door as I come in at the front, all except the cook which tried to take refuge somewhere else.

"Come outa there and fry me some bacon!" I commanded, kicking a few slats out of the counter to add point to my request. It disgusts me to see a grown man trying to hide under a stove. I am a very patient and good-natured human, but Grizzly Claw was getting under my hide. So the cook come out and fried me a mess of bacon and ham and aigs and pertaters and sourdough bread and beans and coffee, and I et three cans of cling peaches. Nobody come into the restaurant whilst I was eating but I thought I heard somebody sneaking around outside.

When I got through I asked the feller how much and he told me, and I planked down the cash, and he commenced to bite it. This lack of faith in his feller humans enraged me, so I drawed my bowie knife and said: "They is a limit to any man's patience! I been insulted once tonight and that's enough! You just dast say that coin's phoney and I'll slice off your whiskers plumb at the roots!"

I brandished my bowie under his nose, and he hollered and stampeded back into the stove and upsot it and fell over it, and the coals went down the back of his shirt, so he riz up and run for the creek yelling bloody murder. And that's how the story started that I tried to burn a cook alive, Indian-style, because he fried my bacon too crisp. Matter of fact, I kept his shack from catching fire and burning down, because I stomped out the coals before they did more'n burn a big hole through the floor, and I throwed the stove out the back door.

It ain't my fault if the mayor of Grizzly Claw was sneaking up the back steps with a shotgun just at that moment. Anyway, I hear he was able to walk with a couple of crutches after a few months.

I emerged suddenly from the front door, hearing a suspicious noise, and I seen a feller crouching close to a side window peeking through a hole in the wall. It was the cowboy I seen in the Apache Queen saloon. He whirled when I come out, but I had him covered.

"Are you spyin' on me?" I demanded. "Cause if you are–"

"No, no!" he said in a hurry. "I was just leanin' up against that wall restin'."

"You Grizzly Claw folks is all crazy," I said disgustedly, and looked around to see if anybody else tried to shoot me, but there warn't nobody in sight, which was suspicious, but I give no heed. It was dark by that time so I went to the wagon-yard, and there wasn't nobody there. I guess the man which run it was off somewheres drunk, because that seemed to be the main occupation of most of them Grizzly Claw devils.

THE ONLY PLACE FOR folks to sleep was a kind of double log-cabin. That is, it had two rooms, but there warn't no door between 'em; and in each room there wasn't nothing but a fireplace and a bunk, and just one outer door. I seen Cap'n Kidd was fixed for the night, and then I went into the cabin and brought in my saddle and bridle and saddle blanket because I didn't trust the people thereabouts. I took off my boots and hat and hung 'em on the wall, and hung my guns and bowie on the end of the bunk, and then spread my saddle-blanket on the bunk and laid down glumly.

I dunno why they don't build them dern things for ordinary sized humans. A man six and a half foot tall like me can't never find one comfortable for him. I laid there and was disgusted at the bunk, and at myself too, because I hadn't accomplished nothing. I hadn't learnt who it was done something to Uncle Jeppard, or what he done. It looked like I'd have to go clean to Bear Creek to find out, and that was a good four days ride.

Well, as I contemplated I heard a man come into the wagon-yard, and purty soon I heard him approach the cabin, but I thought nothing of it. Then the door begun to open, and I riz up with a gun in each hand and said: "Who's there? Make yourself knowed before I blasts you down!"

Whoever it was mumbled some excuse about being on the wrong side, and the door closed. But the voice sounded kind of familiar, and the fellow didn't go into the other room. I heard his footsteps sneaking off, and I riz and went to the door, and looked over toward the row of stalls. So purty soon a man led the pinto out of his stall, and swung aboard him and rode off. It was purty dark, but if us folks on Bear Creek didn't have eyes like a hawk, we'd never live to get grown. I seen it was the cowboy I'd seen in the Apache Queen and outside the restaurant. Once he got clear of the wagon-yard, he slapped in the spurs and went racing through the village like they was a red war-party on his trail. I could hear the beat of his horse's hoofs fading south down the rocky trail after he was out of sight.

I knowed he must of follered me to the wagon-yard, but I couldn't make no sense out of it, so I went and laid down on the bunk again. I was just about to go to sleep, when I was woke by the sounds of somebody coming into the other room of the cabin, and I heard somebody strike a match. The bunk was built against the partition wall, so they was only a few feet from me, though with the log wall between us.

They was two of them, from the sounds of their talking.

"I tell you," one of them was saying, "I don't like his looks. I don't believe he's what he pertends to be. We better take no chances, and clear out. After all, we can't stay here forever. These people are beginnin' to git suspicious, and if they find out for shore, they'll be demandin' a cut in the profits, to protect us. The stuff's all packed and ready to jump at a second's notice. Let's run for it tonight. It's a wonder nobody ain't never stumbled on to that hide-out before now."

"Aw," said the other'n, "these Grizzly Claw yaps don't do nothin' but swill licker and gamble and think up swindles to work on such strangers as is unlucky enough to wander in here. They never go into the hills southwest of the village where our cave is. Most of 'em don't even know there's a path past that big rock to the west."

"Well, Bill," said t'other'n, "we've done purty well, countin' that job up in the Bear Creek country."

At that I was wide awake and listening with both ears.

Bill laughed. "That was kind of funny, warn't it, Jim?" he said.

"You ain't never told me the particulars," said Jim. "Did you have any trouble?"

"Well," said Bill. "T'warn't to say easy. That old Jeppard Grimes was a hard old nut. If all Injun fighters was like him, I feel plumb sorry for the Injuns."

"If any of them Bear Creek devils ever catch you—" begun Jim.

Bill laughed again.

"Them hill-billies never strays more'n ten miles from Bear Creek," he said. "I had the sculp and was gone before they knowed what was up. I've collected bounties for wolves and b'ars, but that's the first time I ever got money for a human sculp!"

A icy chill run down my spine. Now I knowed what had happened to poor old Uncle Jeppard! Scalped! After all the Indian scalps he'd lifted! And them cold-blooded murderers could set there and talk about it, like it was the ears of a coyote or a rabbit!

"I told him he'd had the use of that sculp long enough," Bill was saying. "A old cuss like him–"

I waited for no more. Everything was red around me. I didn't stop for my boots, gun nor nothing, I was too crazy mad even to know such things existed. I riz up from that bunk and put my head down and rammed that partition wall like a bull going through a rail fence.

THE DRIED MUD POURED out of the chinks and some of the logs give way, and a howl went up from the other side.

"What's that?" hollered one, and t'other'n yelled: "Look out! It's a b'ar!"

I drawed back and rammed the wall again. It caved inwards and I come headlong through it in a shower of dry mud and splinters, and somebody shot at me and missed. They was a lighted lantern setting on a hand-hewn table, and two men about six feet tall each that hollered and let *bam* at me with their six-shooters. But they was too dumfounded to shoot straight. I gathered 'em to my bosom and we went backwards over the table, taking it and the lantern with us, and you ought to of heard them critters howl when the burning ile splashed down their necks.

It was a dirt floor so nothing caught on fire, and we was fighting in the dark, and they was hollering: "Help! Murder! We are bein' 'sassinated! Release go my ear!" And then one of 'em got his boot heel wedged in my mouth, and whilst I was twisting it out with one hand, the other'n tore out of his shirt which I was gripping with t'other hand, and run out the door. I had hold of the other feller's foot and commenced trying to twist it off, when he wrenched his laig outa the boot, and took it on the run. When I started to foller him I fell over the table in the dark and got all tangled up in it.

I broke off a leg for a club and rushed to the door, and just as I got to it a whole mob of folks come surging into the wagon-yard with torches and guns and dogs and a rope, and they hollered: "There he is, the murderer, the outlaw, the counterfeiter, the house-burner, the mule-killer!"

I seen the man that owned the mule, and the restaurant feller, and the barkeeper and a lot of others. They come roaring and bellering up to the door, hollering, "Hang him! Hang him! String the murderer up!" And they begun shooting at me, so I fell amongst 'em with my table-leg and laid right and left till it busted. They was packed so close together I laid out three and four at a lick and they hollered something awful. The torches was all knocked down and trompled out except them which was held by fellers which danced around on the edge of the mill, hollering: "Lay hold on him! Don't be scared of the big hill-billy! Shoot him! Knock him in the head!" The dogs having more sense than the men, they all run off except one big mongrel that looked like a wolf, and he bit the mob often'er he did me.

They was a lot of wild shooting and men hollering: "Oh, I'm shot! I'm kilt! I'm dyin'!" and some of them bullets burnt my hide they come so close, and the flashes singed my eye-lashes, and somebody broke a knife against my belt buckle. Then I seen the torches was all gone except one, and my club was broke, so I bust right through the mob, swinging right and left with my fists and stomping on them that tried to drag me down. I got clear of everybody except the man with the torch who was so excited he was jumping up and down trying to shoot me without cocking his gun. That blame dog was snapping at my heels, so I swung him by the tail and hit the man over the head with him. They went down in a heap and the torch went out, and the dog clamped on the feller's ear and he let out a squall like a steam-whistle.

They was milling in the dark behind me, and I run straight to Cap'n Kidd's stall and jumped on him bareback with nothing but a hackamore on him. Just as the mob located where I went, we come storming out of the stall like a hurricane and knocked some of 'em galley-west and run over some more, and headed for the gate. Somebody shut the gate but Cap'n Kidd took it in his stride, and we was gone into the darkness before they knowed what hit them.

Cap'n Kidd decided then was a good time to run away, like he usually does, so he took to the hills and run through bushes and clumps of trees trying to scrape me off on the branches. When I finally pulled him up he was maybe a mile south of the village, with Cap'n Kidd no bridle nor saddle nor blanket, and me with no guns, knife, boots nor hat. And what was worse, them devils which scalped Uncle Jeppard had got away from me, and I didn't know where to look for 'em.

I SET MEDITATING WHETHER to go back and fight the whole town of Grizzly Claw for my boots and guns, or what to do, when all at once I remembered what Bill and Jim had said about a cave and a path running to it. I thought: I bet them fellers will go back and get their horses and pull out, just like they was planning, and they had stuff in the cave, so that's the place to look for 'em. I hoped they hadn't already got the stuff, whatever it was, and gone.

I knowed where that rock was, because I'd seen it when I come into town that afternoon–a big rock that jutted up above the trees about a mile to the west of Grizzly Claw. So I started out through the brush, and before long I seen it looming up against the stars, and I made straight for it. Sure enough, there was a narrow trail winding around the base and leading off to the southwest. I follered it, and when I'd went nearly a mile, I come to a steep mountain-side, all clustered with brush.

When I seen that I slipped off and led Cap'n Kidd off the trail and tied him back amongst the trees. Then I crope up to the cave which was purty well masked with bushes. I listened, but everything was dark and still, but all at once, away down the trail, I heard a burst of shots, and what sounded like a lot of horses running. Then everything was still again, and I quick ducked into the cave, and struck a match.

There was a narrer entrance that broadened out after a few feet, and the cave run straight like a tunnel for maybe thirty steps, about fifteen foot wide, and then it made a bend. After that it widened out and got to be purty big–fifty feet wide at least, and I couldn't tell how far back into the mountain it run. To the left the wall was very broken and notched with ledges, might nigh like stair-steps, and when the match went out, away up above me I seen some stars which meant that there was a cleft in the wall or roof away up on the mountain somewheres.

Before the match went out, I seen a lot of junk over in a corner covered up with a tarpaulin, and when I was fixing to strike another match I heard men coming up the trail outside. So I quick clumb up the broken wall and laid on a ledge about ten feet up and listened.

From the sounds as they arriv at the cave mouth, I knowed it was two men on foot, running hard and panting loud. They rushed into the cave and made the turn, and I heard 'em fumbling around. Then a light flared up and I seen a lantern being lit and hung up on a spur of rock.

In the light I seen them two murderers, Bill and Jim, and they looked plumb delapidated. Bill didn't have no shirt on and the other'n was wearing just one boot and limped. Bill didn't have no gun in his belt neither, and both was mauled and bruised, and scratched, too, like they'd been running through briars.

"Look here," said Jim, holding his head which had a welt on it which was likely made by my fist. "I ain't certain in my mind as to just what all *has* happened. Somebody must of hit me with a club some time tonight, and things is happened too fast for my addled wits. Seems like we been fightin' and runnin' all night. Listen, *was* we settin' in the wagon-yard shack talkin' peaceable, and *did* a grizzly b'ar bust through the wall and nigh slaughter us?"

"That's plumb correct," said Bill. "Only it warn't no b'ar. It was some kind of a human critter—maybe a escaped maneyack. We ought to of stopped for our horses—"

"I warn't thinkin' 'bout no horses," broke in Jim. "When I found myself outside that shack my only thought was to cover ground, and I done my best, considerin' that I'd lost a boot and that critter had nigh unhinged my hind laig. I'd lost you in the dark, so I made for the cave, knowin' you would come there eventually, and it seemed like I was forever gettin' through the woods, crippled like I was. I'd no more'n hit the path when you come up it on the run."

"Well," said Bill, "as I went over the wagon-yard wall a lot of people come whoopin' through the gate, and I thought they was after us, but they must of been after the feller we fought, because as I run I seen him layin' into 'em right and left. After I'd got over my panic, I went back after our horses, but I run right into a gang of men on horseback, and one of 'em was that durned feller which passed hisself off as a cowboy. I didn't need no more. I took out through the woods as hard as I could pelt, and they hollered. 'There he goes!' and come hot-foot after me."

"And was them the fellers I shot at back down the trail?" asked Jim.

"Yeah," said Bill. "I thought I'd shooken 'em off, but just as I seen you on the path, I heard horses comin' behind us, so I hollered to let 'em have it, and you did."

"Well, I didn't know who it was," said Jim. "I tell you, my head's buzzin' like a circle-saw."

"Well," said Bill, "we stopped 'em and scattered 'em. I dunno if you hit anybody in the dark, but they'll be mighty cautious about comin' up the trail. Let's clear out."

"On foot?" said Jim. "And me with just one boot?"

"How else?" said Bill. "We'll have to hoof it till we can steal us some broncs. We'll have to leave all this stuff here. We daren't go back to Grizzly Claw after our horses. I *told* you that durned cowboy would do to watch. He ain't no cowpoke at all. He's a blame detective."

"What's that?" broke in Jim.

"Horses' hoofs!" exclaimed Bill, turning pale. "Here, blow out that lantern! We'll climb the ledges and get out of the cleft, and take out over the mountain where they can't foller with horses, and then–"

IT WAS AT THAT INSTANT that I launched myself offa the ledge on top of 'em. I landed with all my two hundred and ninety pounds square on Jim's shoulders and when he hit the ground under me he kind of spread out like a toad when you step on him. Bill give a scream of astonishment and when I riz and come for him, he tore off a hunk of rock about the size of a man's head and lammed me over the ear with it. This irritated me, so I taken him by the neck, and also taken away a knife which he was trying to hamstring me with, and begun sweeping the floor with his carcass.

Presently I paused and kneeling on him, I strangled him till his tongue lolled out, betwixt times hammering his head against the rocky floor.

"You murderin' devil!" I gritted between my teeth. "Before I varnish this here rock with your brains, tell me why you taken my Uncle Jeppard's scalp!"

"Let up!" he gurgled, being purple in the face where he warn't bloody. "They was a dude travelin' through the country and collectin' souvenirs, and he heard about that sculp and wanted it. He hired me to go git it for him."

I was so shocked at that cold-bloodedness that I forgot what I was doing and choked him nigh to death before I remembered to ease up on him.

"Who was he?" I demanded. "Who is the skunk which hires old men murdered so's he can collect their scalps? My God, these Eastern dudes is worse'n Apaches! Hurry up and tell me, so I can finish killin' you."

But he was unconscious; I'd squoze him too hard. I riz up and looked around for some water or whiskey or something to bring him to so he could tell who hired him to scalp Uncle Jeppard, before I twisted his head off, which was my earnest intention of doing, when somebody said: "Han's up!"

I whirled and there at the crook of the cave stood that cowboy which had spied on me in Grizzly Claw, with ten other men. They all had their Winchesters p'inted at me, and the cowboy had a star on his buzum.

"Don't move!" he said. "I'm a Federal detective, and I arrest you for manufactorin' counterfeit money."

"What you mean?" I snarled, backing up to the wall.

"You know," he said, kicking the tarpaulin off the junk in the corner. "Look here, men! All the stamps and dyes he used to make phoney coins and bills! All packed up, ready to light out. I been hangin' around Grizzly Claw for days, knowin' that whoever was passin' this stuff made his, or their, headquarters here somewheres. Today I spotted that dollar you give the barkeep, and I went *pronto* for my men which was camped back in the hills a few miles. I thought you was settled in the wagon-yard for the night, but it seems you give us the slip. Put the cuffs on him, men!"

"No, you don't!" I snarled, bounding back. "Not till I've finished these devils on the floor. I dunno what you're talkin' about, but–"

"Here's a couple of corpses!" hollered one of the men. "He kilt a couple of fellers!"

One of them stooped over Bill, but he had recovered his senses, and now he riz up on his elbows and give a howl. "Save me!" he bellered. "I confesses! I'm a counterfeiter, and so is Jim there on the floor! We surrenders, and you got to pertect us!"

"*YOU'RE* THE COUNTERFEITERS?" said the detective, took aback as it were. "Why, I was follerin' this giant! I seen him pass fake money myself. We got to the wagon-yard awhile after he'd run off, but we seen him duck in the woods not far from there, and we been chasin' him. He opened fire on us down the trail while ago–"

"That was us," said Bill. "It was me you was chasin'. He musta found that money, if he had fake stuff. I tell you, we're the men you're after, and you got to pertect us! I demands to be put in the strongest jail in this state, which even this here devil can't bust into!"

"And he ain't no counterfeiter?" said the detective.

"He ain't nothin' but a man-eater," said Bill. "Arrest us and take us out of his reach."

"*No!*" I roared, clean beside myself. "They belongs to me! They scalped my uncle! Give 'em knives or gun or somethin' and let us fight it out."

"Can't do that," said the detective. "They're Federal prisoners. If you got any charge against them, they'll have to be indicted in the proper form."

His men hauled 'em up and handcuffed 'em and started to lead 'em out.

"Blast your souls!" I raved. "Does you mean to pertect a couple of dirty scalpers? I'll–"

I started for 'em and they all p'inted their Winchesters at me.

"Keep back!" said the detective. "I'm grateful for you leadin' us to this den, and layin' out these criminals for us, but I don't hanker after no battle in a cave with a human grizzly like you."

Well, what could a feller do?

If I'd had my guns, or even my knife, I'd of taken a chance with the whole eleven, officers or not, I was that crazy mad. But even I can't fight eleven .45-90's with my bare hands. I stood speechless with rage whilst they filed out, and then I went for Cap'n Kidd in a kind of a daze. I felt wuss'n a horse-thief. Them fellers would be put in the pen safe out of my reach, and Uncle Jeppard's scalp was unavenged! It was awful. I felt like bawling.

Time I got my horse back onto the trail, the posse with their prisoners was out of sight and hearing. I seen the only thing to do was to go back to Grizzly Claw and get my outfit, and then foller the posse and try to take their prisoners away from 'em someway.

Well, the wagon-yard was dark and still. The wounded had been carried away to have their injuries bandaged, and from the groaning that was still coming from the shacks and cabins along the street, the casualties had been plenteous. The citizens of Grizzly Claw must have been shook up something terrible, because they hadn't even stole my guns and saddle and things yet; everything was in the cabin just like I'd left 'em.

I put on my boots, hat and belt, saddled and bridled Cap'n Kidd and sot out on the road I knowed the posse had taken. But they had a long start on me, and when daylight come I hadn't overtook 'em. But I did meet somebody else. It was Tunk Willoughby riding up the trail, and when he seen me he grinned all over his battered features.

"Hey, Breck!" he said. "After you left I sot on that log and thunk, and thunk, and I finally remembered what Jack Gordon told me, and I started out to find you again and tell you. It was this: he said to keep a close lookout for a fellow from Grizzly Claw named Bill Jackson, which had gypped yore Uncle Jeppard in a deal."

"*What?*" I said.

"Yeah," said Tunk. "He bought somethin' from Jeppard and paid him in counterfeit money. Jeppard didn't know it was phoney till after the feller had plumb got away," said Tunk, "and bein' as he was too busy dryin' some b'ar meat to go after him, he sent word for you to git him."

"But the scalp–" I said wildly.

"Oh," said Tunk, "that was what Jeppard sold the feller. It was the scalp Jeppard took offa old Yeller Eagle the Comanche war-chief forty years ago, and been keepin' for a souvenear. Seems like a Eastern dude heard about it and wanted to buy it, but this Jackson must of kept the money he give him to git it with, and give Jeppard phoney cash. So you see everything's all right, even if I did forget a little, and no harm did–"

And that's why Tunk Willoughby is going around saying I am a homicidal maneyack, and run him five miles down a mountain and tried to kill him–which is a exaggeration, of course. I wouldn't of kilt him if I could of caught him. I would merely of raised a few knots on his head and tied his hind laigs in a bow-knot around his fool neck and done a few other little things that might of improved his memory.

THE END

War On Bear Creek

Pap dug the nineteenth buckshot out of my shoulder and said, "Pigs is more disturbin' to the peace of a community than scandal, divorce, and corn licker put together. And," says pap, pausing to strop his bowie on my scalp where the hair was all burnt off, "when the pig is a razorback hawg, and is mixed up with a lady schoolteacher, a English tenderfoot, and a passle of bloodthirsty relatives, the result is appallin' for a peaceable man to behold. Hold still till John gits yore ear sewed back on."

Pap was right. I warn't to blame for what happened. Breaking Joel Gordon's laig was a mistake, and Erath Elkins is a liar when he says I caved in them five ribs of his'n plumb on purpose. If Uncle Jeppard Grimes had been tending to his own business he wouldn't have got the seat of his britches filled with bird-shot, and I don't figger it was my fault that cousin Bill Kirby's cabin got burned down. And I don't take no blame for Jim Gordon's ear which Jack Grimes shot off, neither. I figger everybody was more to blame than I was, and I stand ready to wipe up the earth with anybody which disagrees with me.

But it was that derned razorback hawg of Uncle Jeppard Grimes' which started the whole mess.

It begun when that there tenderfoot come riding up the trail with Tunk Willoughby, from War Paint. Tunk ain't got no more sense than the law allows, but he shore showed good jedgement that time, because having delivered his charge to his destination, he didn't tarry. He merely handed me a note, and p'inted dumbly at the tenderfoot, whilst holding his hat reverently in his hand meanwhile.

"What you mean by that there gesture?" I ast him rather irritably, and he said: "I doffs my sombrero in respect to the departed. Bringin' a specimen like that onto Bear Creek is just like heavin' a jackrabbit to a pack of starvin' loboes."

He hove a sigh and shook his head, and put his hat back on. "Rassle a cat in pieces," he says, gathering up the reins.

"What the hell are you talkin' about?" I demanded.

"That's Latin," he said. "It means rest in peace."

And with that he dusted it down the trail and left me alone with the tenderfoot which all the time was setting his cayuse and looking at me like I was a curiosity or something.

I called my sister Ouachita to come read that there note for me, which she did and it run as follows:

Dere Breckinridge:

This will interjuice Mr. J. Pembroke Pemberton a English sportsman which I met in Frisco recent. He was disapinted because he hadn't found no adventures in America and was fixin to go to Aferker to shoot liuns and elerfants but I perswaded him to come with me because I knowed he would find more hell on Bear Creek in a week than he would find in a yere in Aferker or any other place. But the very day we hit War Paint I run into a old ackwaintance from Texas I will not speak no harm of the ded but I wish the son of a buzzard had shot me somewheres besides in my left laig which already had three slugs in it which I never could get cut out. Anyway I am lade up and not able to come on to Bear Creek with J. Pembroke Pemberton. I am dependin on you to show him some good bear huntin and other excitement and pertect him from yore relatives I know what a awful responsibility I am puttin on you but I am askin' this as yore frend.

William Harrison Glanton. Esqy.

I looked J. Pembroke over. He was a medium sized young feller and looked kinda soft in spots. He had yaller hair and very pink cheeks like a gal; and he had on whip-cord britches and tan riding boots which was the first I ever seen. And he had on a funny kinda coat with pockets and a belt which he called a shooting jacket, and a big hat like a mushroom made outa cork with a red ribbon around it. And he had a pack-horse loaded with all kinds of plunder, and four or five different kinds of shotguns and rifles.

"So yo're J. Pembroke," I says, and he says, "Oh, rahther! And you, no doubt, are the person Mr. Glanton described to me, Breckinridge Elkins?"

"Yeah," I said. "Light and come in. We got b'ar meat and honey for supper."

"I say," he said, climbing down. "Pardon me for being a bit personal, old chap, but may I ask if your—ah—magnitude of bodily stature is not a bit unique?"

"I dunno," I says, not having the slightest idee what he was talking about. "I always votes a straight Democratic ticket, myself."

He started to say something else, but just then pap and my brothers John and Bill and Jim and Buckner and Garfield come to the door to see what the noise was about, and he turned pale and said faintly: "I beg your pardon; giants seem to be the rule in these parts."

"Pap says men ain't what they was when he was in his prime," I said, "but we manage to git by."

Well, J. Pembroke laid into them b'ar steaks with a hearty will, and when I told him we'd go after b'ar next day, he ast me how many days travel it'd take till we got to the b'ar country.

"Heck!" I said. "You don't have to travel to git b'ar in these parts. If you forgit to bolt yore door at night yo're liable to find a grizzly sharin' yore bunk before mornin'. This here'n we're eatin' was ketched by my sister Ellen there whilst tryin' to rob the pig-pen out behind the cabin last night."

"My word!" he says, looking at her peculiarly. "And may I ask, Miss Elkins, what caliber of firearm you used?"

"I knocked him in the head with a wagon tongue," she said, and he shook his head to hisself and muttered: "Extraordinary!"

J. PEMBROKE SLEPT IN my bunk and I took the floor that night; and we was up at daylight and ready to start after the b'ar. Whilst J. Pembroke was fussing over his guns, pap come out and pulled his whiskers and shook his head and said: "That there is a perlite young man, but I'm afeared he ain't as hale as he oughta be. I just give him a pull at my jug, and he didn't gulp but one good snort and like to choked to death."

"Well," I said, buckling the cinches on Cap'n Kidd, "I've done learnt not to jedge outsiders by the way they takes their licker on Bear Creek. It takes a Bear Creek man to swig Bear Creek corn juice."

"I hopes for the best," sighed pap. "But it's a dismal sight to see a young man which cain't stand up to his licker. Whar you takin' him?"

"Over toward Apache Mountain," I said. "Erath seen a exter big grizzly over there day before yesterday."

"Hmmmm!" says pap. "By pecooliar coincidence the schoolhouse is over on the side of Apache Mountain, ain't it, Breckinridge?"

"Maybe it is and maybe it ain't," I replied with dignerty, and rode off with J. Pembroke ignoring pap's sourcastic comment which he hollered after me: "Maybe they is a connection between book-larnin' and b'ar-huntin', but who am I to say?"

J. Pembroke was a purty good rider, but he used a funny looking saddle without no horn nor cantle, and he had the derndest gun I ever seen. It was a double-barrel rifle, and he said it was a elerfant-gun. It was big enough to knock a hill down. He was surprised I didn't tote no rifle and ast me what would I do if we met a b'ar. I told him I was depending on him to shoot it, but I said if it was necessary for me to go into action, my six-shooter was plenty.

"My word!" says he. "You mean to say you can bring down a grizzly with a shot from a pistol?"

"Not always," I said. "Sometimes I have to bust him over the head with the butt to finish him."

He didn't say nothing for a long time after that.

Well, we rode over on the lower slopes of Apache Mountain, and tied the horses in a holler and went through the bresh on foot. That was a good place for b'ars, because they come there very frequently looking for Uncle Jeppard Grimes' pigs which runs loose all over the lower slopes of the mountain.

But just like it always is when yo're looking for something, we didn't see a cussed b'ar.

The middle of the evening found us around on the south side of the mountain where they is a settlement of Kirbys and Grimeses and Gordons. Half a dozen families has their cabins within a mile of each other, and I dunno what in hell they want to crowd up together that way for, it would plumb smother me, but pap says they was always peculiar that way.

We warn't in sight of the settlement, but the schoolhouse warn't far off, and I said to J. Pembroke: "You wait here a while and maybe a b'ar will come by. Miss Margaret Ashley is teachin' me how to read and write, and it's time for my lesson."

I left J. Pembroke setting on a log hugging his elerfant-gun, and I strode through the bresh and come out at the upper end of the run which the settlement was at the other'n, and school had just turned out and the chillern was going home, and Miss Ashley was waiting for me in the log schoolhouse.

That was the first school that was ever taught on Bear Creek, and she was the first teacher. Some of the folks was awful sot agen it at first, and said no good would come of book larning, but after I licked six or seven of them they allowed it might be a good thing after all, and agreed to let her take a whack at it.

Miss Margaret was a awful purty gal and come from somewhere away back East. She was setting at her hand-made desk as I come in, ducking my head so as not to bump it agen the top of the door and perlitely taking off my coonskin cap. She looked kinda tired and discouraged, and I said: "Has the young'uns been raisin' any hell today, Miss Margaret?"

"Oh, no," she said. "They're very polite—in fact I've noticed that Bear Creek people are always polite except when they're killing each other. I've finally gotten used to the boys wearing their bowie knives and pistols to school. But somehow it seems so futile. This is all so terribly different from everything to which I've always been accustomed. I get discouraged and feel like giving up."

"You'll git used to it," I consoled her. "It'll be a lot different once yo're married to some honest reliable young man."

She give me a startled look and said: "Married to someone here on Bear Creek?"

"Shore," I said, involuntarily expanding my chest under my buckskin shirt. "Everybody is just wonderin' when you'll set the date. But le's git at the lesson. I done learnt the words you writ out for me yesterday."

But she warn't listening, and she said: "Do you have any idea of why Mr. Joel Grimes and Mr. Esau Gordon quit calling on me? Until a few days ago one or the other was at Mr. Kirby's cabin where I board almost every night."

"Now don't you worry none about them," I soothed her. "Joel'll be about on crutches before the week's out, and Esau can already walk without bein' helped. I always handles my relatives as easy as possible."

"You fought with them?" she exclaimed.

"I just convinced 'em you didn't want to be bothered with 'em," I reassured her. "I'm easy-goin', but I don't like competition."

"Competition!" Her eyes flared wide open and she looked at me like she never seen me before. "Do you mean, that you—that I—that—"

"Well," I said modestly, "everybody on Bear Creek is just wonderin' when you're goin' to set the day for us to git hitched. You see gals don't stay single very long in these parts, and—hey, what's the matter?"

Because she was getting paler and paler like she'd et something which didn't agree with her.

"Nothing," she said faintly. "You—you mean people are expecting me to marry you?"

"Shore," I said.

She muttered something that sounded like "My God!" and licked her lips with her tongue and looked at me like she was about ready to faint. Well, it ain't every gal which has a chance to get hitched to Breckinridge Elkins, so I didn't blame her for being excited.

"You've been very kind to me, Breckinridge," she said feebly. "But I—this is so sudden—so unexpected—I never thought—I never dreamed-"

"I don't want to rush you," I said. "Take yore time. Next week will be soon enough. Anyway, I got to build us a cabin, and—"

Bang! went a gun, too loud for a Winchester.

"Elkins!" It was J. Pembroke yelling for me up the slope. "Elkins! Hurry!"

"Who's that?" she exclaimed, jumping to her feet like she was working on a spring.

"Aw," I said in disgust, "it's a fool tenderfoot Bill Glanton wished on me. I reckon a b'ar is got him by the neck. I'll go see."

"I'll go with you!" she said, but from the way Pembroke was yelling I figgered I better not waste no time getting to him, so I couldn't wait for her, and she was some piece behind me when I mounted the lap of the slope and met him running out from amongst the trees. He was gibbering with excitement.

"I winged it!" he squawked. "I'm sure I winged the blighter! But it ran in among the underbrush and I dared not follow it, for the beast is most vicious when wounded. A friend of mine once wounded one in South Africa, and — "

"A b'ar?" I ast.

"No, no!" he said. "A wild boar! The most vicious brute I have ever seen! It ran into that brush there!"

"Aw, they ain't no wild boars in the Humbolts," I snorted. "You wait here. I'll go see just what you did shoot."

I seen some splashes of blood on the grass, so I knowed he'd shot *something*. Well, I hadn't gone more'n a few hunderd feet and was just out of sight of J. Pembroke when I run into Uncle Jeppard Grimes.

Uncle Jeppard was one of the first white men to come into the Humbolts. He's as lean and hard as a pine-knot, and wears fringed buckskins and moccasins just like he done fifty years ago. He had a bowie knife in one hand and he waved something in the other'n like a flag of revolt, and he was frothing at the mouth.

"The derned murderer!" he howled. "You see this? That's the tail of Daniel Webster, the finest derned razorback boar which ever trod the Humbolts! That danged tenderfoot of your'n tried to kill him! Shot his tail off, right spang up to the hilt! He cain't muterlate my animals like this! I'll have his heart's blood!"

And he done a war-dance waving that pig-tail and his bowie and cussing in English and Spanish and Apache Injun an at once.

"You ca'm down, Uncle Jeppard," I said sternly. "He ain't got no sense, and he thought Daniel Webster was a wild boar like they have in Aferker and England and them foreign places. He didn't mean no harm."

"No harm!" said Uncle Jeppard fiercely. "And Daniel Webster with no more tail onto him than a jackrabbit!"

"Well," I said, "here's a five dollar gold piece to pay for the dern hawg's tail, and you let J. Pembroke alone."

"Gold cain't satisfy honor," he said bitterly, but nevertheless grabbing the coin like a starving man grabbing a beefsteak. "I'll let this outrage pass for the time. But I'll be watchin' that maneyack to see that he don't muterlate no more of my prize razorbacks."

And so saying he went off muttering in his beard.

I WENT BACK TO WHERE I left J. Pembroke, and there he was talking to Miss Margaret which had just come up. She had more color in her face than I'd saw recent.

"Fancy meeting a girl like you here!" J. Pembroke was saying.

"No more surprising than meeting a man like you!" says she with a kind of fluttery laugh.

"Oh, a sportsman wanders into all sorts of out-of-the-way places," says he, and seeing they hadn't noticed me coming up, I says: "Well, J. Pembroke, I didn't find yore wild boar, but I met the owner."

He looked at me kinda blank, and said vaguely: "Wild boar? *What* wild boar?"

"That-un you shot the tail off of with that there fool elerfant gun," I said. "Listen: next time you see a hawg-critter you remember there ain't no wild boars in the Humbolts. They is critters called haverleeners in South Texas, but they ain't even none of them in Nevada. So next time you see a hawg, just reflect that it's merely one of Uncle Jeppard Grimes' razorbacks and refrain from shootin' at it."

"Oh, quite!" he agreed absently, and started talking to Miss Margaret again.

So I picked up the elerfant gun which he'd absent-mindedly laid down, and said: "Well, it's gittin' late. Let's go. We won't go back to pap's cabin tonight, J. Pembroke. We'll stay at Uncle Saul Garfield's cabin on t'other side of the Apache Mountain settlement."

As I said, them cabins was awful close together. Uncle Saul's cabin was below the settlement, but it warn't much over three hundred yards from cousin Bill Kirby's cabin where Miss Margaret boarded. The other cabins was on t'other side of Bill's, mostly, strung out up the run, and up and down the slopes.

I told J. Pembroke and Miss Margaret to walk on down to the settlement whilst I went back and got the horses.

They'd got to the settlement time I catched up with 'em, and Miss Margaret had gone into the Kirby cabin, and I seen a light spring up in her room. She had one of them new-fangled ile lamps she brung with her, the only one on Bear Creek. Candles and pine chunks was good enough for us folks. And she'd hanged rag things over the winders which she called curtains. You never seen nothing like it, I tell you she was that elegant you wouldn't believe it.

29

We walked on toward Uncle Saul's, me leading the horses, and after a while J. Pembroke says: "A wonderful creature!"

"You mean Daniel Webster?" I ast.

"No!" he said. "No, no, I mean Miss Ashley."

"She shore is," I said. "She'll make me a fine wife."

He whirled like I'd stabbed him and his face looked pale in the dusk.

"You?" he said, "*You* a wife?"

"Well," I said bashfully, "she ain't sot the day yet, but I've shore sot my heart on that gal."

"Oh!" he says, "*Oh!*" says he, like he had the toothache. Then he said kinda hesitatingly: "Suppose—er, just suppose, you know! Suppose a rival for her affections should appear? What would you do?"

"You mean if some dirty, low-down son of a mangy skunk was to try to steal my gal?" I said, whirling so sudden he staggered backwards.

"*Steal my gal?*" I roared, seeing red at the mere thought. "Why, I'd— I'd—"

Words failing me I wheeled and grabbed a good-sized sapling and tore it up by the roots and broke it acrost my knee and throwed the pieces clean through a rail fence on the other side of the road.

"That there is a faint idee!" I said, panting with passion.

"That gives me a very good conception," he said faintly, and he said nothing more till we reached the cabin and seen Uncle Saul Garfield standing in the light of the door combing his black beard with his fingers.

NEXT MORNING J. PEMBROKE seemed like he'd kinda lost interest in b'ars. He said all that walking he done over the slopes of Apache Mountain had made his laig muscles sore. I never heard of such a thing, but nothing that gets the matter with these tenderfeet surprizes me much, they is such a effemernate race, so I ast him would he like to go fishing down the run and he said all right.

But we hadn't been fishing more'n a hour when he said he believed he'd go back to Uncle Saul's cabin and take him a nap, and he insisted on going alone, so I stayed where I was and ketched me a nice string of trout.

I went back to the cabin about noon, and ast Uncle Saul if J. Pembroke had got his nap out.

"Why, heck," said Uncle Saul. "I ain't seen him since you and him started down the run this mornin'. Wait a minute—yonder he comes from the other direction."

Well, J. Pembroke didn't say where he'd been all morning, and I didn't ast him, because a tenderfoot don't generally have no reason for anything he does.

We et the trout I ketched, and after dinner he perked up a right smart and got his shotgun and said he'd like to hunt some wild turkeys. I never heard of anybody hunting anything as big as a turkey with a shotgun, but I didn't say nothing, because tenderfeet is like that.

So we headed up the slopes of Apache Mountain, and I stopped by the schoolhouse to tell Miss Margaret I probably wouldn't get back in time to take my reading and writing lesson, and she said: "You know, until I met your friend, Mr. Pembroke, I didn't realize what a difference there was between men like him, and—well, like the men on Bear Creek."

"I know," I said. "But don't hold it agen him. He means well. He just ain't got no sense. Everybody cain't be smart like me. As a special favor to me, Miss Margaret, I'd like for you to be exter nice to the poor sap, because he's a friend of my friend Bill Glanton down to War Paint."

"I will, Breckinridge," she replied heartily, and I thanked her and went away with my big manly heart pounding in my gigantic bosom.

Me and J. Pembroke headed into the heavy timber, and we hadn't went far till I was convinced that somebody was follering us. I kept hearing twigs snapping, and oncet I thought I seen a shadowy figger duck behind a bush. But when I run back there, it was gone, and no track to show in the pine needles. That sort of thing would of made me nervous, anywhere else, because they is a awful lot of people which would like to get a clean shot at my back from the bresh, but I knowed none of them dast come after me in my own territory. If anybody was trailing us it was bound to be one of my relatives and to save my neck I couldn't think of no reason why anyone of 'em would be gunning for me.

But I got tired of it, and left J. Pembroke in a small glade while I snuck back to do some shaddering of my own. I aimed to cast a big circle around the opening and see could I find out who it was, but I'd hardly got out of sight of J. Pembroke when I heard a gun bang.

I turned to run back and here come J. Pembroke yelling: "I got him! I got him! I winged the bally aborigine!"

He had his head down as he busted through the bresh and he run into me in his excitement and hit me in the belly with his head so hard he bounced back like a rubber ball and landed in a bush with his riding boots brandishing wildly in the air.

"Assist me, Breckinridge!" he shrieked. "Extricate me! They will be hot on our trail!"

"Who?" I demanded, hauling him out by the hind laig and setting him on his feet.

"The Indians!" he hollered, jumping up and down and waving his smoking shotgun frantically. "The bally redskins! I shot one of them! I saw him sneaking through the bushes! I saw his legs! I know it was an Indian because he had on moccasins instead of boots! Listen! That's him now!"

"A Injun couldn't cuss like that," I said. "You've shot Uncle Jeppard Grimes!"

TELLING HIM TO STAY there, I run through the bresh, guided by the maddened howls which riz horribly on the air, and busting through some bushes I seen Uncle Jeppard rolling on the ground with both hands clasped to the rear bosom of his buckskin britches which was smoking freely. His langwidge was awful to hear.

"Air you in misery, Uncle Jeppard?" I inquired solicitously. This evoked another ear-splitting squall.

"I'm writhin' in my death-throes," he says in horrible accents, "and you stands there and mocks my mortal agony! My own blood-kin!" he says. "ae-ae-ae-ae!" says Uncle Jeppard with passion.

"Aw," I says, "that there bird-shot wouldn't hurt a flea. It cain't be very deep under yore thick old hide. Lie on yore belly, Uncle Jeppard," I said, stropping my bowie on my boot, "and I'll dig out them shot for you."

"Don't tech me!" he said fiercely, painfully climbing onto his feet. "Where's my rifle-gun? Gimme it! Now then, I demands that you bring that English murderer here where I can git a clean lam at him! The Grimes honor is besmirched and my new britches is rooint. Nothin' but blood can wipe out the stain on the family honor!"

"Well," I said, "you hadn't no business sneakin' around after us thataway—"

Here Uncle Jeppard give tongue to loud and painful shrieks.

"Why shouldn't I?" he howled. "Ain't a man got no right to pertect his own property? I was follerin' him to see that he didn't shoot no more tails offa my hawgs. And now he shoots me in the same place! He's a fiend in human form—a monster which stalks ravelin' through these hills bustin' for the blood of the innercent!"

"Aw, J. Pembroke thought you was a Injun," I said.

"He thought Daniel Webster was a wild wart-hawg," gibbered Uncle Jeppard. "He thought I was Geronimo. I reckon he'll massacre the entire population of Bear Creek under a misapprehension, and you'll uphold and defend him! When the cabins of yore kinfolks is smolderin' ashes, smothered in the blood of yore own relatives, I hope you'll be satisfied—bringin' a foreign assassin into a peaceful community!"

Here Uncle Jeppard's emotions choked him, and he chawed his whiskers and then yanked out the five-dollar gold piece I give him for Daniel Webster's tail, and throwed it at me.

"Take back yore filthy lucre," he said bitterly. "The day of retribution is close onto hand, Breckinridge Elkins, and the Lord of battles shall jedge between them which turns agen their kinfolks in their extremerties!"

"In their which?" I says, but he merely snarled and went limping off through the trees, calling back over his shoulder: "They is still men on Bear Creek which will see justice did for the aged and helpless. I'll git that English murderer if it's the last thing I do, and you'll be sorry you stood up for him, you big lunkhead!"

I went back to where J. Pembroke was waiting bewilderedly, and evidently still expecting a tribe of Injuns to bust out of the bresh and sculp him, and I said in disgust: "Let's go home. Tomorrer I'll take you so far away from Bear Creek you can shoot in any direction without hittin' a prize razorback or a antiquated gunman with a ingrown disposition. When Uncle Jeppard Grimes gits mad enough to throw away money, it's time to ile the Winchesters and strap your scabbard-ends to yore laigs."

"Legs?" he said mistily, "But what about the Indian?"

"There warn't no Injun, gol-dern it!" I howled. "They ain't been any on Bear Creek for four or five year. They—aw, hell! What's the use? Come on. It's gittin' late. Next time you see somethin' you don't understand, ast me before you shoot it. And remember, the more ferocious and woolly it looks, the more likely it is to be a leadin' citizen of Bear Creek."

It was dark when we approached Uncle Saul's cabin, and J. Pembroke glanced back up the road, toward the settlement, and said: "My word, is it a political rally? Look! A torchlight parade!"

I looked, and I said: "Quick! Git into the cabin and stay there."

He turned pale, and said: "If there is danger, I insist on—"

"Insist all you dern please," I said. "But git in that house and stay there. I'll handle this. Uncle Saul, see he gits in there."

Uncle Saul is a man of few words. He taken a firm grip on his pipe stem and grabbed J. Pembroke by the neck and seat of the britches and throwed him bodily into the cabin, and shet the door, and sot down on the stoop.

"They ain't no use in you gittin' mixed up in this, Uncle Saul," I said.

"You got yore faults, Breckinridge," he grunted. "You ain't got much sense, but yo're my favorite sister's son—and I ain't forgot that lame mule Jeppard traded me for a sound animal back in '69. Let 'em come!"

* * * *

THEY COME ALL RIGHT, and surged up in front of the cabin—Jeppard's boys Jack and Buck and Esau and Joash and Polk County. And Erath Elkins, and a mob of Gordons and Buckners and Polks, all more or less kin to me, except Joe Braxton who wasn't kin to any of us, but didn't like me because he was sweet on Miss Margaret. But Uncle Jeppard warn't with 'em. Some had torches and Polk County Grimes had a rope with a noose in it.

"Where-at air you all goin' with that there lariat?" I ast them sternly, planting my enormous bulk in their path.

"Perjuice the scoundrel!" said Polk County, waving his rope around his head. "Bring out the foreign invader which shoots hawgs and defenseless old men from the bresh!"

"What you aim to do?" I inquired.

"We aim to hang him!" they replied with hearty enthusiasm.

Uncle Saul knocked the ashes out of his pipe and stood up and stretched his arms which looked like knotted oak limbs, and he grinned in his black beard like a old timber wolf, and he says: "Whar is dear cousin Jeppard to speak for hisself?"

"Uncle Jeppard was havin' the shot picked outa his hide when we left," says Joel Gordon. "He'll be along directly. Breckinridge, we don't want no trouble with you, but we aims to have that Englishman."

"Well," I snorted, "you all cain't. Bill Glanton is trustin' me to return him whole of body and limb, and—"

"What you want to waste time in argyment for, Breckinridge?" Uncle Saul reproved mildly. "Don't you know it's a plumb waste of time to try to reason with the off-spring of a lame-mule trader?"

"What would you suggest, old man?" sneeringly remarked Polk County.

Uncle Saul beamed on him benevolently, and said gently: "I'd try moral suasion—like this!" And he hit Polk County under the jaw and knocked him clean acrost the yard into a rain barrel amongst the ruins of which he reposed until he was rescued and revived some hours later.

But they was no stopping Uncle Saul oncet he took the war-path. No sooner had he disposed of Polk County than he jumped seven foot into the air, cracked his heels together three times, give the rebel yell and come down with his arms around the necks of Esau Grimes and Joe Braxton, which he went to the earth with and starting mopping up the cabin yard with 'em.

That started the fight, and they is no scrap in the world where mayhem is committed as free and fervent as in one of these here family rukuses.

Polk County had hardly crashed into the rain barrel when Jack Grimes stuck a pistol in my face. I slapped it aside just as he fired and the bullet missed me and taken a ear offa Jim Gordon. I was scared Jack would hurt somebody if he kept on shooting reckless that way, so I kinda rapped him with my left fist and how was I to know it would dislocate his jaw. But Jim Gordon seemed to think I was to blame about his ear because he give a maddened howl and jerked up his shotgun and let *bam* with both barrels. I ducked just in time to keep from getting my head blowed off, and catched most of the double-charge in my shoulder, whilst the rest hived in the seat of Steve Kirby's britches. Being shot that way by a relative was irritating, but I controlled my temper and merely taken the gun away from Jim and splintered the stock over his head.

In the meantime Joel Gordon and Buck Grimes had grabbed one of my laigs apiece and was trying to rassle me to the earth, and Joash Grimes was trying to hold down my right arm, and cousin Pecos Buckner was beating me over the head from behind with a ax-handle, and Erath Elkins was coming at me from the front with a bowie knife. I reached down and got Buck Grimes by the neck with my left hand, and I swung my right and hit Erath with it, but I had to lift Joash clean off his feet and swing him around with the lick, because he wouldn't let go, so I only knocked Erath through the rail fence which was around Uncle Saul's garden.

About this time I found my left laig was free and discovered that Buck Grimes was unconscious, so I let go of his neck and begun to kick around with my left laig and it ain't my fault if the spur got tangled up in Uncle Jonathan Polk's whiskers and jerked most of 'em out by the roots. I shaken Joash off and taken the ax-handle away from Pecos because I seen he was going to hurt somebody if he kept on swinging it around so reckless, and I dunno why he blames me because his skull got fractured when he hit that tree. He oughta look where he falls when he gets throwed across a cabin yard. And if Joel Gordon hadn't been so stubborn trying to gouge me he wouldn't of got his laig broke neither.

I was handicapped by not wanting to kill any of my kinfolks, but they was so mad they all wanted to kill me, so in spite of my carefulness the casualties was increasing at a rate which would of discouraged anybody but Bear Creek folks. But they are the stubbornnest people in the world. Three or four had got me around the laigs again, refusing to be convinced that I couldn't be throwed that way, and Erath Elkins, having pulled hisself out of the ruins of the fence, come charging back with his bowie.

By this time I seen I'd have to use violence in spite of myself, so I grabbed Erath and squoze him with a grizzly-hug and that was when he got them five ribs caved in, and he ain't spoke to me since. I never seen such a cuss for taking offense over trifles.

For a matter of fact, if he hadn't been so bodaciously riled up—if he had of kept his head like I did—he would have seen how kindly I felt toward him even in the fever of that there battle. If I had dropped him underfoot he might have been tromped on fatally for I was kicking folks right and left without caring where they fell. So I carefully flung Erath out of the range of that ruckus—and if he thinks I aimed him at Ozark Grimes and his pitchfork—well, I just never done it. It was Ozark's fault more than mine for toting that pitchfork, and it ought to be Ozark that Erath cusses when he starts to sit down these days.

It was at this moment that somebody swung at me with a ax and ripped my ear nigh offa my head, and I begun to lose my temper. Four or five other relatives was kicking and hitting and biting at me all at oncet, and they is a limit even to my timid manners and mild nature. I voiced my displeasure with a beller of wrath, and lashed out with both fists, and my misguided relatives fell all over the yard like persimmons after a frost. I grabbed Joash Grimes by the ankles and begun to knock them ill-advised idjits in the head with him, and the way he hollered you'd of thought somebody was manhandling him. The yard was beginning to look like a battle-field when the cabin door opened and a deluge of b'iling water descended on us.

I got about a gallon down my neck, but paid very little attention to it, however the others ceased hostilities and started rolling on the ground and hollering and cussing, and Uncle Saul riz up from amongst the ruins of Esau Grimes and Joe Braxton, and bellered: "Woman! What air you at?"

Aunt Zavalla Garfield was standing in the doorway with a kettle in her hand, and she said: "Will you idjits stop fightin'? The Englishman's gone. He run out the back door when the fightin' started, saddled his nag and pulled out. Now will you born fools stop, or will I give you another deluge? Land save us! What's that light?"

Somebody was yelling toward the settlement, and I was aware of a peculiar glow which didn't come from such torches as was still burning. And here come Medina Kirby, one of Bill's gals, yelping like a Comanche.

"Our cabin's burnin'!" she squalled. "A stray bullet went through the winder and busted Miss Margaret's ile lamp!"

WITH A YELL OF DISMAY I abandoned the fray and headed for Bill's cabin, follered by everybody which was able to foller me. They had been several wild shots fired during the melee and one of 'em must have hived in Miss Margaret's winder. The Kirbys had dragged most of their belongings into the yard and some was bringing water from the creek, but the whole cabin was in a blaze by now.

"Whar's Miss Margaret?" I roared.

"She must be still in there!" shrilled Miss Kirby. "A beam fell and wedged her door so we couldn't open it, and —"

I grabbed a blanket one of the gals had rescued and plunged it into the rain barrel and run for Miss Margaret's room. They wasn't but one door in it, which led into the main part of the cabin, and was jammed like they said, and I knowed I couldn't never get my shoulders through either winder, so I just put down my head and rammed the wall full force and knocked four or five logs outa place and made a hole big enough to go through.

The room was so full of smoke I was nigh blinded but I made out a figger fumbling at the winder on the other side. A flaming beam fell outa the roof and broke acrost my head with a loud report and about a bucketful of coals rolled down the back of my neck, but I paid no heed.

I charged through the smoke, nearly fracturing my shin on a bedstead or something, and enveloped the figger in the wet blanket and swept it up in my arms. It kicked wildly and fought and though its voice was muffled in the blanket I ketched some words I never would of thought Miss Margaret would use, but I figgered she was hysterical. She seemed to be wearing spurs, too, because I felt 'em every time she kicked.

By this time the room was a perfect blaze and the roof was falling in and we'd both been roasted if I'd tried to get back to the hole I knocked in the oppersite wall. So I lowered my head and butted my way through the near wall, getting all my eyebrows and hair burnt off in the process, and come staggering through the ruins with my precious burden and fell into the arms of my relatives which was thronged outside.

"I've saved her!" I panted. "Pull off the blanket! Yo're safe, Miss Margaret!"

"ae-ae-ae-ae-ae!" said Miss Margaret, and Uncle Saul groped under the blanket and said: "By golly, if this is the schoolteacher she's growed a remarkable set of whiskers since I seen her last!"

He yanked off the blanket—to reveal the bewhiskered countenance of Uncle Jeppard Grimes!

"Hell's fire!" I bellered. "What *you* doin' here?"

"I was comin' to jine the lynchin', you blame fool!" he snarled. "I seen Bill's cabin was afire so I clumb in through the back winder to save Miss Margaret. She was gone, but they was a note she'd left. I was fixin' to climb out the winder when this maneyack grabbed me."

"Gimme that note!" I bellered, grabbing it. "Medina! Come here and read it for me."

That note run:

Dear Breckinridge:

I am sorry, but I can't stay on Bear Creek any longer. It was tough enough anyway, but being expected to marry you was the last straw. You've been very kind to me, but it would be too much like marrying a grizzly bear. Please forgive me. I am eloping with J. Pembroke Pemberton. We're going out the back window to avoid any trouble, and ride away on his horse. Give my love to the children. We are going to Europe on our honeymoon.

With love.

Margaret Ashley.

"Now what you got to say?" sneered Uncle Jeppard.

"I'm a victim of foreign entanglements," I said dazedly. "I'm goin' to chaw Bill Glanton's ears off for saddlin' that critter on me. And then I'm goin' to lick me a Englishman if I have to go all the way to Californy to find one."

Which same is now my aim, object and ambition. This Englishman took my girl and ruined my education, and filled my neck and spine with burns and bruises. A Elkins never forgets?and the next one that pokes his nose into the Bear Creek country had better be a fighting fool or a powerful fast runner.

THE END